DIAMOND DREAMS

BY CYRANO DE WORDS-U-LAC

D0905659

Diamond Dreams
ISBN 1-88144-181-3
Copyright © 1996 Dan and Dave Davidson
Rhymeo Ink
P.O. Box 1416
Salem, Virginia 24153
Application has been made for a registered federal trademark for "Rhymeo" and "Show-It Poet."

Published by Trade Life
P.O. Box 55325
Tulsa, Oklahoma 74155

WHAT'S A RHYMEO™?

Rhymeos™ are fat-free un-poetry — lite and lean literary cuisine. Rhymeos™ are short and sketchy, quick and catchy — two short lines reinforced in rhyme. Although the short rhyming couplets display a poetic flavor, they are not traditional poetry. They are actually jingles about life — Jingle Verse Poetry for the 21st Century — offering insight and motivation, humor and inspiration.

Cyrano De Words-u-lac pens the shortest verse in the universe — a story to tell in a nutshell, a rhyming report to make a long story short. Rhymeos™ are short and sweet and poetically petite — clever ways to paraphrase — bite-sized words to the wise. Whether concise advice or an easy doesy fuzzy wuzzy, Rhymeos™ give a reflective perspective in a fireside chat format. It's literary rap with a snap — poetically correct dialect — a way to cope with humor and hope!

D I A M O N D
D R E A M S

Field Diamond Dream
Career Dream — **What** you want to be . . .
—represented by a young child dreaming of being a major leaguer.

Gem Diamond Dream
Character Dream — **How** you want to be . . .
—represented by qualities of a perfect gemstone - purity, value, and virtue.

Ring Diamond Dream
Candlelight Dream — **Who** you want to be with . . .
—represented by our dreams of relationships in friendship and marriage.

The Grand Plow Plan
Five Steps To Redeem and Harvest Diamond Dreams

T h i n k   W O W   D i a m o n d   D r e a m s
Dare to dream to the extreme.

M a k e   a   V O W   D i a m o n d   D e v o t i o n
Commit your heart before you start.

P l a n   H O W   D i a m o n d   D e t a i l s
Design a grand how-to plan.

D o   i t   N O W   D i a m o n d   D e e d s
Start somehow to do it now.

P u s h   t h e   P L O W   D i a m o n d   D i l i g e n c e
Daily be diligent and persistent.

EDISON EDGE
Grand Plow Plan Pledge™

I am willing to be rejected or fail
up to 1000 times before I prevail.

Thomas Alva Edison had over **1,800** failures before he found the right filament for the light bulb. He never quit or gave up, but rather saw failures as stepping stones to future success. Colonel Sanders had a devoted vision for a chicken recipe in his retirement. He faced **1,003** rejections before his first chicken recipe deal. The word grand means one thousand. The *Edison Edge Grand Plow Plan Pledge™* is for those who are willing to be rejected or fail up to a minimum of 1000 times before a diamond dream is fulfilled.

This important *VOW* stage of the *Grand Plow Plan™* involves a level of commitment that enables us to keep our hands persistently pressed to the plow. The *WOW* of a *Diamond Dream* and the *VOW* of *Diamond Devotion* coupled with the *HOW* of *Diamond Details* and the *NOW* of *Diamond Deeds* leads to the *PLOW* of *Diamond Diligence* creating a dynamic power that fuels, pulls, and drives us toward Diamond Dream fulfillment.

DIAMOND DREAMS

THINK WOW

JOIN THE SELECT
OF BUYING DIRECT.

•••

MAKE EACH DECISION
BASED ON A VISION.

DARE TO DREAM
TO THE EXTREME.

KEEP ON THE GO
AS YOUR OWN CEO.

♦♦♦

NURTURE YOUR NICHE
TO BECOME RICH.

LEARN TO BE CONTENT DURING DREAM FULFILLMENT.

DON'T ALWAYS GO
WITH THE STATUS QUO.

•••

AVOID THE POSITION
OF SELFISH AMBITION.

BUILD SELF-ESTEEM
WITHIN A TEAM.

ALWAYS AFFIRM
GOALS LONG–TERM.

•••

DON'T HESITATE
TO INITIATE.

AS A PRIORITY PURSUE WHAT'S IMPORTANT TO YOU.

BE A TRAIL BLAZER
AND A PEOPLE PRAISER.

•••

DON'T MAKE EXCUSES WITH
"IF ONLY" AND "WHAT IF."

DON'T LET YOUR DREAMS BE GET-RICH-QUICK SCHEMES.

∙∙∙Diamond∙Dreams∙∙∙

DEVELOP A THIRST
FOR FIRST THINGS FIRST.

∙∙∙

SQUEEZE THE TRIGGER
OF THINKING BIGGER.

WORK TO BE
AN M.V.P.

···DIAMOND◆DREAMS···

BE A PIONEER
AND OPEN A FRONTIER.

◆◆◆

ALWAYS PLAN
TO EXPAND.

CASH IN AND CAPITALIZE ON A PRIVATE FRANCHISE.

DIVERSIFY
TO KEEP INCOME HIGH.

•◆•

START WHERE YOU ARE
AND PLAN TO GO FAR.

⋯◆DIAMOND◆DREAMS◆⋯

DON'T LET OTHERS STEAL DREAMS YOU REVEAL.

DO YOUR PART
TO MAKE A START.

◆◆◆

TRY A NEW PARADIGM
FROM TIME TO TIME.

EARN A PROFIT
PERCENT
OF WHAT OTHERS
HAVE SPENT.

ENERGIZE
FREE ENTERPRISE.

•••

SHUN THE PITCHES
OF GET-QUICK-RICHES.

STEP OUT AND LEAD
TO HELP OTHERS SUCCEED.

DON'T EVER LET
YOUR HEART REGRET.

•••

SET GOALS THAT ARE LOFTY
AND DON'T BE A SOFTY.

TAKE THE CHANCE
ON A CAREER ADVANCE.

•••DIAMOND•DREAMS•••

ALWAYS ASK
FOR THE NEXT TASK.

•••

LISTEN AND LEARN
FOR WAYS TO EARN.

SAY, "ENOUGH IS ENOUGH" AND GET OFF YOUR DUFF.

✦✦✦ DIAMOND ✦ DREAMS ✦✦✦

SHARE AND ESTEEM
THE AMERICAN DREAM.

✦✦✦

RISE ABOVE AND SOAR
OFF THE GROUND FLOOR.

DIAMOND DEVOTION

MAKE A VOW

◆◆◆ Diamond ◆ Dreams ◆◆◆

DISPLAY DEVOTION
IN EVERY PROMOTION.

◆◆◆

PUT SOME CELEBRATION
IN YOUR OPERATION.

COMMIT YOUR HEART
BEFORE YOU START.

EDUCATE
TO REPLICATE.

•◆•

DON'T LET YOUR GROUP
START TO DROOP.

BE A FANTASTIC
ENTHUSIASTIC.

DREAM EVERY DAY
REGARDLESS OF RESUME .

•••

PLAY THE LEAD ROLE
IN YOUR GOAL.

ALWAYS INVEST
IN WHAT STANDS THE TEST.

ENDORSE
YOUR SALES FORCE.

•••

DON'T EVER BE A JERK
WITH YOUR WORK.

TAKE AN OATH
FOR PERSONAL GROWTH.

CLAIM A CREED
TO NOT MISLEAD.

•••

PUT PEP IN YOUR STEP
AS A COMPANY REP.

WALK
YOUR TALK.

PURSUE
WHAT IS TRUE.

•◆•

WRITE DOWN THE MISSION
OF YOUR AMBITION.

DIAMOND DETAILS

PLAN HOW

CATEGORY INVENTORY.

•••

SCHEDULE PRIME WORK TIME.

DESIGN A GRAND HOW-TO PLAN.

ADD PERSPIRATION
TO YOUR INSPIRATION.

•••

AIM FOR ASCENSION
AT A CONVENTION.

BE WILLING TO FAIL
1000 TIMES TO PREVAIL.

•••DIAMOND•DREAMS•••

OFFER CREATIVE
SPONSOR INCENTIVE.

•◆•

TRACK DOLLARS AND CENTS
FOR BUSINESS EXPENSE.

HAVE THE UPPER HAND ON SUPPLY AND DEMAND.

ALWAYS ENDURE
AS AN ENTREPRENEUR.

•◆•

MAKE UP YOUR MIND
TO NOT GET BEHIND.

BUILD A GOOD FOUNDATION WITH DOMINO DUPLICATION.

IMPLEMENT
A COMPLIMENT.

•◆•

FOLLOW THE GOLDEN RULE,
NOT THE FOLLY OF A FOOL.

DELEGATE AND DESIGN
NEW WAYS TO STREAMLINE.

STEER CLEAR
OF PHONE FEAR.

❖❖❖

DON'T BE STUFFY
OR TOO FLUFFY.

ALWAYS TRY
TO MULTIPLY.

✦✦✦ Diamond Dreams ✦✦✦

SELL HOUSEHOLD GOODS
TO IMPROVE LIVELIHOODS.

✦✦✦

PROCLAIM EACH PERK
OF A NETWORK.

LIVE BY A BUDGET
AND DON'T FUDGE IT.

ALWAYS COMPLETE
THE SALES RECEIPT.

•❖•

CUT THE MIDDLEMAN
OUT WHEN YOU CAN.

SELL AND SIGN
DOWN THE LINE.

LEARN LESSONS
ASKING QUESTIONS.

◆◆◆

REMEMBER HONESTY
IS THE BEST POLICY.

TAP THE STRENGTH FROM A BUSINESS TWOSOME.

TARGET
YOUR MARKET.

•◆•

DON'T POKE FUN
AT ANYONE.

INCREASE THE SUM
OF RESIDUAL INCOME.

USE POLITE SPEECH
WHEN TIME TO BESEECH.

◆◆◆

DON'T BE BLINDED
OR CLOSE MINDED.

GET OTHERS INVOLVED
IN PROBLEMS TO BE SOLVED.

EMPATHIZE,
DON'T SYMPATHIZE.

•❖•

TEACH TEAM TRUST
AS A MUST.

DON'T MAKE ROOM
FOR DOOM AND GLOOM.

DON'T BE THE TYPE
TO HOUND ON HYPE.

✦✦✦

KEEP THE LEAD
TO SUCCEED.

FIGURE IN EACH FACTOR AS A SOLO CONTRACTOR.

BE PRECISE
WITH THE PRICE.

◆◆◆

PLAN TO PRESENT
AT A LOCAL EVENT.

DON'T BE A FOOL
FOR A BUSY SCHEDULE.

START A BUSINESS PLAN
WITH LITTLE CASH ON HAND.

•••

BOOST THE BOTTOM LINE
DIAMOND DOLLAR SIGN.

INTRODUCE AND INVITE ALL WHO MIGHT BE RIGHT.

BE BRAVE
AND MAKE A WAVE.

•◆•

TRADE IN DOLLARS PER HOUR
FOR DUPLICATION POWER.

KNOW ALL ABOUT
DISPELLING DOUBT.

ALWAYS BE SURE
TO LOG AN EXPENDITURE.

•••

SAVE PART OF YOUR WAGE
FOR RETIREMENT AGE.

+++DIAMOND+DREAMS+++

AIM YOUR ARROW
STRAIGHT AND NARROW.

REPORT ALL PROFIT
WITH OR WITHOUT AN AUDIT.

•••

KEEP AND COORDINATE
PRIORITIES STRAIGHT.

REPRODUCE AND REAP, EVEN WHILE YOU SLEEP.

EXPAND
WITH NAME BRAND.

✦✦✦

NETWORK WITH PEERS
FOR 2–5 YEARS.

DIAMOND DEEDS

D O   I T   N O W

INVEST IN THE BEST
CLIENT, CONTACT, OR GUEST.

•◆•

PREPARE FOR AN INFLUX
OF NEW PRODUCTS.

START SOMEHOW
TO DO IT NOW.

BE AN EXCEPTION
TO SALES DECEPTION.

◆◆◆

SHOW AND TELL
TO EXCEL.

SPOON FEED
AND PLANT A SEED.

OPEN AND UNLOCK OPPORTUNITY'S KNOCK.

❖❖❖

HELP OTHERS UNDERSTAND THE BUSINESS PLAN.

MAKE COINS CLANK
IN A PIGGY BANK.

TRY HARDER
TO BE A SELF-STARTER.

•••

BE A BIG ORDER
REWARDER.

WORRY LESS
AND LIMIT STRESS.

STAY ON THE BALL
WITH A FOLLOW-UP CALL.

◆◆◆

TURN AN EXPRESSION
INTO A QUESTION.

SHOW OTHERS A SAMPLE
OF SUCCESS BY EXAMPLE.

UTILIZE THE COURSE
OF HUMAN RESOURCE.

•◆•

STARE DOWN FEAR
IN THE MIRROR.

FOLLOW THROUGH
WITH YOUR TO-DO.

REPLACE A RUDE ATTITUDE
WITH GRACE AND GRATITUDE.

•••

PERSIST AND PERFORM
TO TAKE BY STORM.

HAVE THE WISDOM
FOR A BACKUP SYSTEM.

TEACH AND TRAIN
TO GO AGAINST THE GRAIN.

•◆•

DON'T EVER LET DEBT
BE YOUR REGRET.

MAKE THE MOVE
TO IMPROVE.

MOTIVATE
AND ACTIVATE.

•••

BE A ONE-ON-ONE
PHENOMENON.

GO THE EXTRA MILE
WITH A SINCERE SMILE.

VOW
TO DO IT NOW.

•••

INCREASE PRODUCTIVITY
TO PROVIDE SECURITY.

STAND UP STRONG
FOR RIGHT AND WRONG.

DECREASE DEBT
WITH A SAFETY NET.

◆◆◆

HELP COUPLES AGREE
TO WORK IN UNITY.

KEEP YOUR WORD
HOW IT WAS HEARD.

ZIP YOUR LIP
TO NIP GOSSIP.

•◆•

SHARE BROCHURES
OF JOINT VENTURES.

EACH MONTH IDENTIFY WHAT CUSTOMERS MAY BUY.

MEET DEADLINES
AND MAKE HEADLINES.

•••

GIVE CREDIT WHERE IT'S DUE;
DON'T DEMAND IT FOR YOU.

NEVER GO WEAK
IN A HOT STREAK.

◆◆◆DIAMOND◆DREAMS◆◆◆

COMMUNICATE
WITH THOSE YOU APPRECIATE.

◆◆◆

STAND IN CUSTOMER'S SHOES
OR CHOOSE TO LOSE.

KNOW WHAT TO SAY AND WHEN TO RELAY.

••• DIAMOND DREAMS •••

MAKE IT YOUR AIM
TO REPEAT A NEW NAME.

•••

RESERVE ADVANCED SEATING
FOR A RALLY MEETING.

DARE
TO SHARE.

HARVEST FRUITS
THROUGH GRASSROOTS.

•◆•

TAKE A VACATION
FOR RELAXATION.

ASSOCIATE
TO DUPLICATE.

ONCE A WEEK RELAX AND
TUNE OUT WHAT DISTRACTS.

•❖•

PASS DOWN COMPENSATION
TO THE NEXT GENERATION.

LET GO
OF YOUR EGO.

MANAGE THE URGE
TO SPEND AND SPLURGE.

◆◆◆

ENCOURAGE AND SHOW
OTHERS HOW TO GROW.

TURN OFF THE TV
AND TUNE IN TO FAMILY.

✦✦✦ Diamond ✦ Dreams ✦✦✦

NEVER CHEAT
ON A SPREADSHEET.

✦✦✦

AT TIMES BE BLUNT
AND UP FRONT.

HAND OUT HOPE
WHEN IT'S HARD TO COPE.

MAKE FAITH A HABIT;
DON'T BREAK IT, GRAB IT.

•••

REGAIN AND RENEW
VIRTUE AND VALUE.

CALL IF RUNNING LATE FOR A BUSINESS DATE.

SEIZE THE DAY
AND DON'T DELAY.

◆◆◆

KNOW WHEN TO CLAIM
THE COMPANY NAME.

DIAMOND DILIGENCE

PUSH THE PLOW

OVERCOME REJECTION
BY HURDLING OBJECTION.

•❖•

DON'T LET OTHERS STEAL
YOUR ZIP AND ZEAL.

DAILY BE DILIGENT AND PERSISTENT.

DO ALL YOU CAN DO
TO PROMOTE VALUE.

•••

IF A PROSPECT SAYS NO,
GIVE IT ANOTHER GO.

MAKE THE SALE
WITHOUT FAIL.

···Diamond◆Dreams···

ASK WHAT YOU CAN DO
FOR THE RED, WHITE, AND BLUE.

◆◆◆

KEEP YOUR EYES
ON THE PRIZE.

ENDEAVOR
TO BE CLEVER.

BUILD UP PERCENT
FOR DIRECT ASCENT.

•••

DON'T BE IN THE FOG
ABOUT A CATALOG.

DEVELOP THE DISCIPLINE OF NOT GIVING UP OR IN.

LIKE A GOLD MINE,
PRESENT THE CORE LINE.

•••

READ AND REVIEW
PLANS TO PURSUE.

HAVE OVER–THE–FENCE
SELF CONFIDENCE.

BE AGGRESSIVE,
BUT NOT OPPRESSIVE.

•◆•

NOURISH YOUR WISH
TO ACCOMPLISH.

WORK TO AVOID
BEING UNEMPLOYED.

SHARE THE PLAN
WHENEVER YOU CAN.

•••

WORK SMARTER,
NOT HARDER.

DON'T LET YOUR FRIENDS STAY STUCK IN DEAD ENDS.

GROW BY GIVING
WHILE EARNING A LIVING.

•◆•

WITH OTHERS EXTEND
A SHARED DIVIDEND.

WORK TO PERSUADE, BUT NEVER INVADE.

BE REFLECTIVE
ON YOUR OBJECTIVE.

•••

REMOVE RESISTANCE
WITH PERSISTENCE.

PRACTICE YOUR PITCH TO FIX A GLITCH.

SEE THE BIG PICTURE AND DON'T BE A FIXTURE.

•◆•

DON'T PRESSURE A FRIEND OR EVER OFFEND.

REMEMBER COMMON
SENSE WHEN TRYING
TO CONVINCE.

•••DIAMOND•DREAMS•••

DO BUSINESS BY THE BOOK
WITH AN OWNERSHIP OUTLOOK.

•◆•

IF AT FIRST YOU DON'T SUCCEED,
PERSEVERE AND PROCEED.

SHOW IT'S VITAL NOT TO BE IDLE.

❖❖❖ Diamond ❖ Dreams ❖❖❖

INSIST AND PERSIST
ON A PROSPECT LIST.

❖❖❖

KNOW THE TIME AND PLACE
TO PRESENT FACE-TO-FACE.

BOOST AND BOOM BUSINESS VOLUME.

REASSURE
YOUR CUSTOMER.

•••

BE A GOPHER,
NOT A LOAFER.

PERSEVERE
WITH YOUR EAR.

OVERCOME FEARS
OF SHARING WITH PEERS.

•••

STAY ON THE RIGHT TRACK
AND DON'T LOOK BACK.

NEVER EVER STOP
EVEN AT THE TOP.

SAY GOOD–BYE
TO BEING SHY.

◆◆◆

GIVE 110 PERCENT
OF YOUR COMMITMENT.

A TALE TO KNOW BY CYRANO
The Inspiration Behind A Legend In His Own Rhymy

Let me share with you a tale of inspiration and betrayal,
a story of poetic word, of my great, great granddad Cyrano de Bergerac.
For he had a tender heart and his nose was a work of art,
as a poet the part he played was that of a romantic serenade.
While another man spoke his prose, granddad hid behind his nose,
as the maiden was swayed by the rhyme of his friend's charade.
Generations later I found out about this hoax behind his snout,
and as a youth I felt betrayed by his phony masquerade.

I became ashamed of this mimicry and the heritage of my family,
but then one day I read by chance, the words he used for romance.
It was then when my heart realized the legacy of my family ties.
I saw him in a new light. My heart was touched, and now I write.
The prose composed from my pen, I propose as a new trend . . .
poetic proverbs known as *Rhymeos*™, by the Show-It Poet™ Cyrano,
Rearranged along this path of fame, was my granddad's last name,
no longer am I called de Bergerac; I am *Cyrano De Words-u-lac.*
If you find your lines are few, the words you lack I'll choose for you.
For I've pledged to become over time . . . a legend in my own rhyme.

WHO IS CYRANO?

a literary
dignitary
a word weaver
Rhymeo™ retriever
a prolific writer
and poetic reciter
among supermen
of the fountain pen

Cyrano De Words-u-lac
is the combined pen name of brothers
Dr. Dan the Man and Dave the Wave Davidson

PARTNERS IN RHYME
the brothers behind Cyrano's mind

More Rhymeo™ Titles
by Cyrano De Words-u-lac

If I Could Live My Life Again

A Mother's Love Is Made Up Of . . .

Home & Heart Improvement For Men

It's Time Again To Skip A Birthday When . . .

If you have a Rhymeo™ for Cyrano send what you've penned to the

Quill Guild ™

for Rhymeo™ Writers, Readers & Friends of Cyrano

Write or call Cyrano to receive a FREE Quill Guild™ Rhymeo™ newsletter
or for information on the **Life Story Inventory™, Grand Plow Plan™**
and **Diamond Dream** workshops.

Rhymeo Ink P.O. Box 1416 Salem , VA 24153
CompuServe - **71175,1035** *Prodigy* - **GCSU92A**
America Online - **rhymeo** *E-mail* - **rhymeo@aol.com**
phone (540) 989-0592 fax (540) 989-6176
1 8 0 0 4 R H Y M E O
visit the Rhymeo™ by Cyrano Web Site on the Internet
http://www.rhymeo.com